Three-Minute Tales

DUCKLINGS

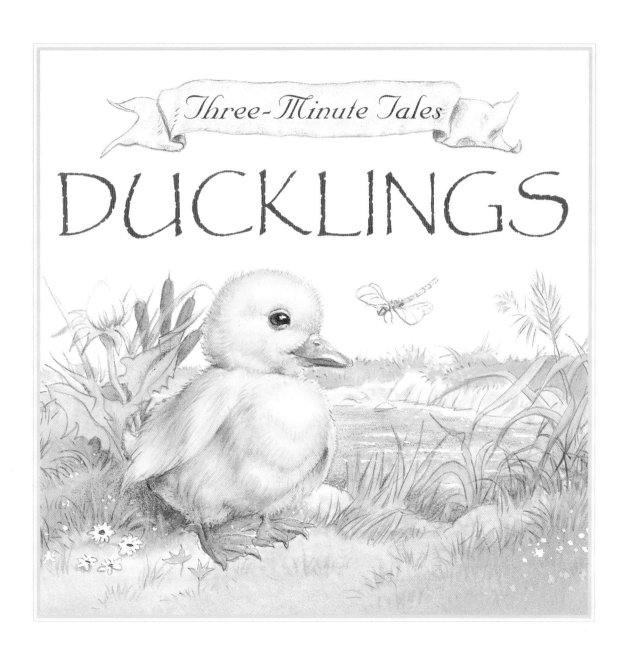

p

This is a Parragon book
First Published in 2000

Parragon
Queen Street House, 4 Queen Street,
Bath, BA1 1HE, UK

Produced by The Templar Company plc
Pippbrook Mill, London Road, Dorking,
Surrey, RH4 1JE, UK

Designed by Kilnwood Graphics

Printed and bound in Spain
ISBN 0 75253 606 0

Three Minute Tales

DUCKLINGS

Written by Caroline Repchuk • Illustrated by Mario Capaldi

CONTENTS

Forever Friends

Like a Duck to Water!

Danny Duckling
In Trouble

"Stay still so I can count!" quacked Mummy Duck crossly, as the little ducklings splashed about. "Just as I thought, Danny's missing again. We'd better go and look for him!" It was the third time that week Danny Duckling had got lost. He liked to swim at the end of the line and often got left behind. But this time he was in trouble...

Earlier that day, Danny had been following along through the reeds when his foot caught in something beneath the water.
"Bother!" he quacked as he tried to pull it free.

He ducked into the water and saw that his foot
was tangled in an old fishing net held fast in
the mud. "Help!" he cried to the others, but
they were already too far away to hear.

The more Danny struggled, the tighter the net gripped his foot. "Help!" he quacked, flapping his fluffy little wings. Luckily, Freya Frog heard his cries and dived under the water to try and free him, but it was no use. "I'll go and get help," she said, swimming off. "Hurry!" Danny called after her. The tide was coming in and the river was rising fast!

By the time Freya returned with Wally Water
Rat, the water was covering Danny's back.
"I'm going to be pulled under!" cried Danny.
"Don't worry," said Wally. "We'll save you!"
In no time at all, Wally's sharp teeth nibbled

through the net, and Danny bobbed back to
the surface just as his Mummy appeared.
"Thank goodness you're safe," said Mummy.
"But from now on swim at the front of the line."
And that is just what Danny did.

ALL AT SEA!

It was a lovely spring day when Dippy Duckling peeked out of her warm nest at the shimmering river. How cool and inviting the water looked. Soon she was swimming along happily, calling out to all the animals that lived on the riverbank as she went by. She didn't realise how fast or how far the current was carrying her as she swept along past forests and fields.

As Dippy floated on enjoying the warm sun on her back Sally Seagull flew by squawking loudly. "I've never seen a bird like that on the river before," thought Dippy, in surprise.

Then just as she came round a great bend in the river she saw the wide shining ocean spread out in front of her! Dippy began to shake with terror — she was going to be swept out to sea!

She started to paddle furiously against the tide, but it was no use. The current was too strong.

Just then, a friendly face popped up nearby. It was Ollie Otter. He was very surprised to find Dippy so far from home. "Climb on my back," he said. Soon his strong legs were pulling them back up the river and safely home.

"Thank you, Ollie," said Dippy. "Without you, I'd be all at sea!"

Forever Friends

Daisy Duckling had lots of friends but her best friend of all was Glenda Gosling. Every day they played together, chasing each other through the reeds. "When I grow up, I'll be a beautiful swan like my mummy!" said Glenda. "And I'll be a dull little brown duck," said Daisy. She worried that Glenda would only want to play with her pretty swan friends when she grew up.

Then one day, they were playing hide and seek
when something dreadful happened.
While Daisy hid amongst some large dock leaves,
a sly fox crept up and snatched her in his mouth!

Before she had time to quack he was heading for his lair. But Glenda had been watching. Without hesitating she rushed after the fox and caught the tip of his long tail in her sharp beak.

As the fox spun round, she pecked him hard on the nose. His mouth dropped open and Daisy fell out. Now he was really mad and rushed at them. But Mrs Duck and Mrs Swan flew at him hissing furiously and off he ran. Daisy couldn't thank them enough. "That's what friends are for!" said Glenda. And Mrs Swan and Mrs Duck, who were the best of friends, could not agree more.

LIKE A DUCK TO WATER

Mrs Duck swam proudly across the farm pond
followed by a line of fluffy ducklings. Hidden in
the safety of the nest Dozy Duckling peeked
out and watched them go. He wished he was
brave enough to go with them but he was afraid
of the water! Instead, he pretended to be asleep,
and Mrs Duck told the others to leave him alone.

When they returned that night they told him tales of all the scary animals they had met by the pond. "There's a big thing with hot breath called Horse," said Dotty. "There's a huge smelly pink thing called Pig," said Dickie.

"But worst of all," said Doris, "there's a great grey bird, called Heron. Pig says he gobbles up little ducklings for breakfast!" At that all the little ducklings squawked with fear and excitement.

Next morning, Mrs Duck hurried the ducklings out for their morning parade.

Dozy kept his eyes shut until they had gone then looked up to see a great grey bird towering over him! He leapt into the water crying, "Help, wait for me!" But the others started laughing! "It's a trick! Heron won't eat you. We just wanted you to come swimming. And you've taken to it like a duck to water!"

The End